Usborne
Illustrated Stories
of
Mermaids

Usborne
Illustrated Stories
of
Mermaids

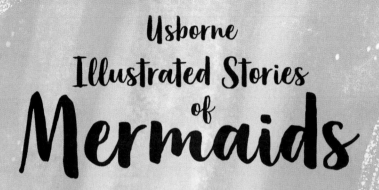

Illustrated by
Margarita Kukhtina

Retold by
Lan Cook, Susanna Davidson,
Rachel Firth and Fiona Patchett

Contents

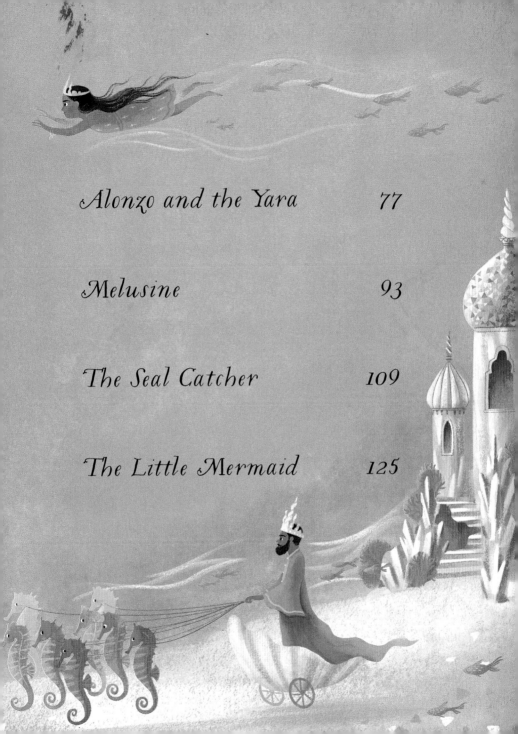

This old folk tale comes from the village of Zennor in Cornwall, at the very southern tip of England.

The Mermaid of Zennor

*T*he bells chimed out, as people crammed
into the church of Saint Senara in Zennor.
Just as they were settling into their seats,
a mysterious woman entered the church. No one
had ever seen her before. The village was a quiet
one, perched on a cliff, high above the sea, and
quite remote from anywhere else in Cornwall.

Not many new people came to the village, so this stranger caused quite a stir. Her eyes were an unusual deep blue that glistened like the sea, and her hair fell down to her waist, like rivers of shining gold over her flowing blue dress. Quietly, she took a seat right at the back of the church, but that did not stop heads turning and voices whispering. *Who is she? Where has she come from?* No one seemed to know.

Young Mathey Trewella was the best singer in the church choir. When the organ began to play, Mathey stood up confidently to sing his solo and the whole church hushed. His voice was rich, deep and spellbinding. As he sang, he noticed the stranger's eyes fixing on him and he thought he saw her smile warmly.

At the chorus, everyone stood up to join in. Mathey could hear the stranger's voice clearly above the others. It rang out like silver bells, creating a perfect harmony with his own. His heart leaped at the beautiful sound their voices made together.

At the end of the service, the stranger came over to Mathey.

"Hello," she said in a soft voice. "What's your name?"

"M-Mathey," he stammered.

"My name is Morveren," she told him. "You have the finest voice I've ever heard."

Mathey blushed, but before he could find the words to reply, Morveren had disappeared into the crowd and out of the church. She was gone!

All week, Mathey could not stop thinking about Morveren. He prayed she would come to church the next week. He longed to sing with her some more.

The following Sunday, the church was packed more than ever. Mathey looked carefully along each row, but he couldn't see Morveren anywhere.

Then, just before the service was about to begin, in she swept and took the same place, right at the back of the church. Again, she gazed admiringly at Mathey as he sang and her own lovely voice blended with his.

From that day on, Morveren came to church every Sunday, always arriving seconds before the service was about to start. And afterwards, before anyone could pin her down and find out who she was, she slipped away like quicksilver.

Mathey became determined to find out more about this mysterious woman with the enchanting singing voice. He thought carefully about what he could do. Then he remembered that there was a small door just behind the choir, which came out on the same side of the church as the main entrance. The next week, as soon as he saw Morveren stand up to leave, he was quick! He bolted from his seat and out through the small side door.

As Mathey emerged into the bright sunlight, there she was, only a few steps ahead of him, hurrying across the churchyard. Mathey ran to catch up with her, but Morveren had already disappeared down a narrow street. Mathey turned into that street too, only in time to see a swish of her blue dress disappear around the corner.

Mathey kept following, as Morveren wound her way through the village, then away across the fields and out of sight completely.

"I've lost her," he thought, sadly. But then he caught another glimpse of the same dazzling blue moving along a wooded path going down to Pendour Cove. The light was glinting off her dress, reminding him of the way it danced off the ripples on the sea. Mathey ran even faster.

Eventually, he came close enough to see her dress was dripping with water. The delicate pattern gleamed as brightly as a silvered fish, darting beneath the surface of the sea.

"Morveren, Morveren, please wait for me," he called in desperation, but again she was slipping away. She reached the rocks right at the edge of the water... and finally he caught up with her.

Morveren turned to look at him with her deep blue eyes.

"Mathey, I cannot stay on the land. I'm... I'm a mermaid. I belong in the sea. I heard your voice from the cove and I had to come to the church to hear you sing, and to see you for myself. But I can't stay any longer. I have to return to the sea."

He looked again at her shimmering dress and saw that it was now a mermaid's tail, made of beautiful, gleaming scales. But still, he couldn't bear to leave her.

"I'll come with you," he said. "Take me to your home under the sea."

"You can't." Morveren shook her head, but he could hear the regret in her voice.

"Please–" he began.

"If you come with me," Morveren interrupted, "you can NEVER go back to the land.

It means leaving your life as a human behind. Do you understand?"

"I *have* to come with you," Mathey replied.

He had never felt more certain of anything in his life.

So Morveren took Mathey's hand firmly in her own and dived into the deep blue water... pulling him down with her.

The people of Zennor never saw nor heard of Morveren or Mathey again. His family was heartbroken. Everyone in the village helped search for him, but they could find no hint of where he had gone. Many years passed and still people wondered what had become of them.

Then, one day, a tall sailing ship anchored just off Pendour Cove. The sailors were busy on deck when they heard the most beautiful voice calling to them from the waves.

*So Morveren took Mathey's hand firmly in her own and dived
into the deep blue water... pulling him down with her.*

They looked overboard and were stunned
to see a mermaid with long golden hair
and deep blue eyes swim right up to the
ship. The sailors had been on many
voyages around the world and had
heard countless tales of mermaids,
but they had never seen one
for themselves.

"Would you mind moving your anchor?" asked the mermaid politely. "It's resting on the door of my house on the seabed. My husband and children are inside and I cannot get back to them."

The sailors had heard enough on their travels to know it is wise always to respect the wishes of mermaids. They happily agreed and moved their anchor. The mermaid thanked them kindly and disappeared beneath the rolling waves.

That evening, the sailors came on shore and told their story, ready to impress the locals in the village inn.

"You'll never believe what happened at Pendour Cove today," said the captain, his voice booming around the inn. "A mermaid with long golden hair and deep blue eyes swam right up to the ship and asked us to move our anchor. Sure as anything."

He knew this sounded a far-fetched tale, but the people of Zennor listened carefully. The description seemed familiar. The mermaid sounded just like Morveren, the mysterious woman who used to come to church and then disappeared with Mathey.

"Go on," they said. "Then what happened?"

"Well, she told us our anchor was resting on her door. She asked if we could move it as her husband and children were inside."

Could her husband possibly be Mathey? They believed he must be. In memory of Morveren and Mathey, the people of Zennor carved a mermaid on a bench in the church. It has been there for hundreds of years now.

If you visit, you will be able to see it right at the back of the church, just where Morveren used to sit. On calm summer nights, people say they can still hear the sweet, happy voices of Morveren and Mathey floating across the sea at Pendour Cove.

This story comes from One Thousand and One Nights, *a collection of folk tales from the Middle East.*

The Sea Princess

The mighty monarch, King Shahriman, lived in the White City, in the Land of the Sun. He had almost everything a king could wish for – wealth, power and a beautiful palace, which lay on the shores of a sparkling sea. But he had great sorrow too, for he had no children to inherit his throne.

One day, as the King strolled through his palace gardens, he saw a woman walking down one of the pathways. She was trailing behind one of the many merchants who came to the palace to sell their wares.

The King took one look at the woman – at her eyes, as bright as stars, and her expression, full of curiosity and wisdom – and fell instantly in love. That very day, he asked her to marry him.

The woman paused for a long time before answering (not something this great and powerful king expected) but, finally, she did say yes. They were married soon after, in a splendid and wonderful wedding, full of feasting, that went on for many days.

Then the King took his new wife to the finest apartments in the palace, with windows that let in the sun and looked out onto the waves. He asked his servants to bring her the richest robes they could find, along with the finest pearl necklaces, the most

sparkling diamonds, the bluest of sapphires. He had
morsels of the most tempting food sent to her rooms –
fragrant rice and soft dates stuffed with walnuts. There
were bowls of jewel-red pomegranates and delicious
halva, made with flour and nuts, toasted in golden
butter, mixed with rosewater, sugar and saffron.

But the King's new wife never spoke a word to him.
Instead, she gazed out of the window at the glittering
sea, or bowed her head, so her long dark hair fell to the
floor in waves, hiding the world from view.

The King didn't know what to do.
He spent a whole year with her,
treasuring each moment.
He devoted himself to her,
lavishing her with gifts
and praise and time,
but still she would
not speak.

"I love you," the King said, at last. "I wish with all my heart that you would talk to me. I think I might soon die if you do not say a word. Why do you not speak?"

His wife looked at him with her bright eyes, and at long last she spoke.

"I am broken-hearted," she said, simply. "I am far from my home and from the family that I love."

The King clutched her hands, overjoyed that she had spoken. "Everything I have is yours," he said. "Let *this* palace, *this* kingdom, be your home. As for your family... only tell me where they are and I will send for them and bring them to you."

"You must listen to the rest of my story first," his wife replied. "My name is Gulnar the Mermaid, and I am sea-born. My father was one of the Kings of the High Seas and my mother is Queen Locust of the Sea. After my father died, another king rose up against us and took over our realm. My brother was worried for my safety, and suggested I leave our Kingdom-Under-the-Sea and head for land. So one night, in great sorrow, I left the sea and sat on the rocks in the moonlight."

She paused, and the King could see the sadness in her eyes.

"But I was no happier on land than I had been under the waves," Gulnar continued. "A merchant found me and brought me to the White City, and your palace. I have longed for my home, and I stayed with you only because you loved me. You won me over with your kindness. Otherwise, I would have leaped from my window straight into the sparkling sea. I have kept silent because I am a poor stranger in a foreign land, parted from my mother and my brother and the home that I love. Would you not have done the same?"

At that, the King went down on one knee, and said how sorry he was for all that she had been through. He was full of wonder, too, his mind bursting with unanswered questions.

"I have heard tales of people who live under the sea," he said. "Told by sailors, sung in songs, whispered in stories... but I had never believed them to be true. Tell me, how do you live under the water? How do you breathe?"

"We breathe the water as you breathe the air," Gulnar replied. "Our people are as different from each other as the creatures on earth. Some have human form, others are half-fish, with fish's tails for legs."

"And where do you live?" asked the King.

"In sumptuous palaces," Gulnar replied, "made of rock-crystal and coral. We have sea horses that

we ride across the sea floor in chariots made of
mother-of-pearl. There are precious stones on the
sea floor, larger and far more plentiful than there are
on earth. We have day and night, as you do; we speak
the same tongue. And even though my people live
beneath the waves, and yours live under the sun,
we are not so very different."

"Gulnar," said the King, repeating
her name. "You were named for the
pomegranate-flower, fiery red. You are
my rose of the sea. What will you
do now? Will you go back to the
Kingdom-Under-the-Sea?"

And as the King asked this last question, his voice trembled a little.

"I will stay here with you," Gulnar replied. "I will give you a child, for I have grown to love you as much as you love me."

The next year, just as she had promised, Gulnar gave birth to a beautiful baby – a boy she named Badr Basim, or Smile-of-the-Moon. The King doted on his new son as much as he doted on his wife.

But then Gulnar told her husband it was time for her to call on her family.

First, she opened the window. Then she lit a little fire, and took two pieces of sweet-smelling wood from the folds of her dress. As the flames flickered and grew, she threw the wood on the fire. Smoke began to plume and curl around the room and the King could only stare in amazement.

Gulnar whispered secret words beneath her

breath that the King could not catch or understand.
But outside the window, he saw the sea begin to swirl
and froth until a young man rose up from the waves.
He was bright as the full moon, with teeth like pearls.
Beside him came an old woman with sea-green hair,
flecked with white. They walked on the surface of
the water, then floated upwards, as light as foam,
in through the wide-open window.

"My brother, the Prince," said Gulnar. "And my
mother, Queen Locust of the Sea."

"Gulnar!" they cried. "At last we have found you!
Where have you been all this time?"

Gulnar told her family her story, of being found
on the rocks and taken to the palace, and of the
goodness shown to her by the King.

"We are glad to see you happy here," said her
brother, "but now it is time for you to come back with
us, to where you belong."

"We have won back our realm," added the Queen. "We live in peace. It is safe for you to return."

But Gulnar shook her head. "I am happy here, for I have everything I need. A home, a husband who loves me and listens to me... and now a son."

As she spoke, she went to fetch her baby and held him out to her brother, who took him in his arms.

Before the King could say a word, the Prince leaped out of the window, still holding Smile-of-the-Moon, and plunged into the sea below.

"My son!" cried the King. "My son!"

"Do not fear," said Gulnar. "He will be back."

The King waited, tensely gazing out of the window. He watched the sea rising and falling, growing more turbulent, bubbling and roiling.

And then, at last, he breathed again, as the waves parted and the Prince returned, Smile-of-the-Moon in his arms, the baby's face glowing like the full moon.

And then, at last, he breathed again, as the waves parted and the Prince returned, Smile-of-the-Moon in his arms...

The Prince handed the baby back to his father. "I have smeared his eyelids with kohl and I have whispered words to him, our secret words, so he need never fear the sea. He will never drown. Just as you walk on land, he will walk in the sea, too. He has our gift. He has his birthright."

Then the Prince and his mother held Gulnar in their arms one more time, and kissed her.

"We hate to leave you," said Queen Locust of the Sea, "but we must return to our kingdom. We will always be here for you."

And on those words, they returned the way they had come, out through the window, floating down to the sea. They walked a little while on the water, then slipped beneath the waves, back to their hidden kingdom.

As for Gulnar and her husband... They lived happily together till the great King breathed his last.

And Smile-of-the-Moon, in turn, became a great king too. Like his father, he fell in love with a princess of the sea, his destiny following him faster than the wind. But that is another story...

This story, about a mermaid called Mama Dlo, *comes from Trinidad and Tobago.*

Mama Dlo

*I*t was dark and mysterious in the forest. Ti Jeanne would listen to the trees, creaking and groaning. Monkeys chattered on high. The undergrowth heaved with hidden life: snakes and spiders, scorpions and toads. But Ti Jeanne knew it wasn't only home to animals. Magical creatures lived there too, ancient as time.

Papa Bois, Father-of-the-Forest, was said to dart between the shadows, as swift as a deer on his cloven hooves. His body was thick with fur and his beard of leaves rustled in the wind. And in the quiet pools and running rivers, in the tumbling streams and deep lagoons, lived Mama Dlo, Mother-of-the-Water. "She's half-woman, half-snake," said Ti Jeanne's grandmother. "Watch out for that one!"

For every day, Ti Jeanne would go down to the forest river, to wash clothes. "Endless clothes and endless washing..." thought Ti Jeanne. She saw her life strung out in front of her, like clothes hung up to dry on a line. Sometimes, she thought she heard the SNAP! of Mama Dlo's scaly tail on the water's surface. Or she would wonder if she'd seen a shape, turning in the water in a forest pool.

"Mama Dlo can be kind, sometimes," Ti Jeanne's grandmother told her. "But if she's angry, then the best thing is to take off your left shoe, turn it upside down, and walk backwards all the way home. That's the only way to escape."

"What makes Mama Dlo angry?"

"Anything that troubles the forest waters," her grandmother replied. "Mama Dlo wants to protect the rivers and the pools and all the creatures that live in them. And sometimes, she takes people, too."

"Takes them?"

"Mmm hmm," said Grandmother. "Those she likes, she takes to be her fairy maids. She gives them fish's tails, and they help her with her work."

Then came a hot, hot day. So hot, that Ti Jeanne walked deeper and deeper into the forest – deeper than she'd ever gone before. She walked with her basket of laundry tucked under her arm, dreaming of the coolness of the river and the shade of the gumbo-limbo trees that grew beside its quiet pools.

Ti Jeanne walked down the sun-dappled paths, parrots squawking overhead, the air thick and humid. When she reached a river pool, she placed her basket on the bank. Then she waded into the water until she was knee-deep, her skirt tucked up, loving the slick cool of the river under the hot sun. She took out the clothes, one by one, and she washed them and she scrubbed them, churning up the water until it was filled with bubbles, gleaming on the water's surface. *Pop!...Pop!...Pop!* they went as she worked.

Ti Jeanne was young, but she was strong. Her arms were round and muscled, and she slapped the clothes against the great, bare rocks and stretched them out to dry. Then she sat on a rock and gazed at her reflection in the still waters, admiring her neat features, turning her head this way and that.

"How pretty I am..." thought Ti Jeanne. *"The queen, the queen, the river queen,"* she sang, while the

sun slowly
slipped down
the sky, and long
shadows gathered
at the pool's edge.

The parrots squawked
among the branches, flying
over her in a riot of yellow and green.
"*Qu'est-ce qu'elle dit?*" tweeted the kiskidee,
"*What's she saying?*" and Ti Jeanne sang on.

"*The queen, the queen, the river queen,*" she repeated,
smiling again at her reflection.

"Who's that singing?" came a voice from the dark
leaves at the edge of the river pool. "Who is that,
singing so fine?"

The voice was old and deep, creaky as the branches
of the gumbo-limbo tree.

"Show yourself!" demanded Ti Jeanne.

A deep, throaty chuckle came in reply.

Ti Jeanne's heart beat with fear. She began to back away, her feet stumbling and splashing through the water. But the voice carried on.

"I see you, washer-woman, admiring yourself in the water, looking this way and that."

"I d-didn't mean any harm," stuttered Ti Jeanne.

Ripples broke out across the water's surface. The dark leaves rustled.

Then slowly, slowly, a face emerged from the water. An old, old face with gleaming gold earrings, big as rocks. Then a neck, strung with beaded necklaces, followed by shoulders, broad and strong.

"Ti Jeanne, Ti Jeanne," the woman sang to her. *"Washer-woman! Washer-woman! Mmmh! Hmmm!"* The old woman was humming now, the sound rising and falling like gentle waves, and Ti Jeanne couldn't look away. She was still full of fear but utterly

entranced, unable to take her eyes from the old woman's face.

"Oh! Mama Dlo!" Ti Jeanne cried, suddenly. For now she could see that this woman, with her old, old face, had a snake's body, thick as an anaconda's, with gleaming silver scales. She knew her for the Mother-of-the-Water, the spirit her grandmother had told her about, many times.

"Did I upset you?" said Ti Jeanne. "Was I wrong to do my laundry in your pool?"

And in that moment, she remembered what her grandmother had taught her: *Take off your left shoe, turn it upside down, and walk backwards all the way home. That's the only way to escape.*

But it was too late for that now. Mama Dlo's eyes were gazing into hers, and she couldn't look away. She wasn't even sure she wanted to.

"Oh! Mama Dlo!" cried Ti Jeanne again.

For now Mama Dlo was high in the air above her, rearing up on her great tail, her whole body swaying...

"Mmmh! Hmmm!" hummed Mama Dlo, the hot air humming with her, so the whole forest seemed to vibrate with her sound.

Ti Jeanne began to sway too, from side to side, keeping time with Mama Dlo, their eyes locked.

"Come here, Ti Jeanne!" croaked Mama Dlo. And, mesmerized, Ti Jeanne came, taking one step forward, then another. The water got deeper and deeper.

Mama Dlo slapped the water with her tail, creating waves that rose higher and higher, foaming the surface with bubbles, as if hundreds of washer-women were at work in that river pool.

The waves washed over Ti Jeanne's knees. She walked deeper still. The waves rose up her legs. Deeper and deeper into the river pool went Ti Jeanne, the waves lapping over her stomach, over her shoulders...

*"Come here, Ti Jeanne!" croaked Mama Dlo.
And, mesmerized, Ti Jeanne came...*

and then they reached Ti Jeanne's lips. She was blowing bubbles of her own now. *Pop!...Pop!...Pop!* they went as the water washed over her head.

Then Ti Jeanne sank down, into the depths of the river pool. Mama Dlo sank with her, smiling and humming as she went. Last of all, *SLAP!* went Mama Dlo's scaly tail on the surface.

Then nothing. Just stillness. No ripples, no sound, no singing: just the sun, slowly sinking into evening, the shadows stretching full and ripe across the river.

The sky turned orange and red, then darkness began to nibble at its corners. A faint breeze stirred the branches of the gumbo-limbo tree. Bats swooped silently overhead.

The moon was full in the sky by the time the villagers came looking for Ti Jeanne. But all they found was the laundry on the rocks, and beside it, seven shiny scales, silver as the stars.

The villagers brought back what they'd found to Ti Jeanne's grandmother, who shook her head.

"Ti Jeanne's been taken by Mama Dlo," she said. "She'll be living as one of her fairy maids now, in the rivers and lakes, with a silver tail all of her own."

And that's exactly how it was... Mama Dlo had taken Ti Jeanne to her river world. The rest of her life would be spent playing with the other water spirits and protecting the forest rivers and pools. She had swapped her legs for a fish's tail, and would never do laundry again.

Stories about merfolk called jiaoren have been told
in China for thousands of years. This one is based
on a story written 300 years ago.

Jing and the Pearls

Standing on the deck of the ship, Jing's heart leaped as he caught sight of land – shadowy mountains, their tops lost in the clouds, rising up beyond the glittering sea. For three years, Jing had been away, studying in a distant city, and now, at last, he was coming home, back to where he belonged.

By the time the boat drew into dock, night had closed in on the little bay. Stars shone down and the moon sat round and full in the sky, casting strange shadows across the rocks.

It was the flapping sound that first drew Jing's attention – something wet and heavy, flip-flopping against the stony beach beside the port. And when Jing looked, he thought it was the light of the moon playing tricks on him, for there was the shape of a man, covered in seaweed, with a fish's tail. Jing shook his head, laughing at himself, thinking he had been at sea for far too long.

As soon as the boat landed, Jing made his way down to the beach for a closer look. "It must be a piece of driftwood," he told himself, "covered in seaweed, with a fish trapped beneath it."

But when he reached the strange shape, he saw his eyes hadn't lied, the moon wasn't playing tricks...

For there, lit by starlight, was a man with seaweed for hair, and a fish's tail, gleaming silver, wetly flapping, mesmerizing to watch.

"Who... What are you?" Jing stammered.

"I'm a merman," the creature replied. "My name is Jiaoren, and I belong in the Kingdom-Under-the-Sea. But I cannot go back there."

"Why not?" asked Jing.

"The King and Queen of the Sea have banished me. I was weaving the finest purple silk for the wedding dress of their daughter, the Mer-Princess. It was going to be such a beautiful dress – a *perfect* dress – but I was working so fast to get it finished on time, that the weaving loom broke.

It is the only loom in the kingdom. I'll never forgive myself, and neither will they. So here I am, washed up on this stony shore, with no work and nowhere to live."

As he spoke, he looked longingly back at the ocean and let out a moan – a low rattling sound, like waves over scattered pebbles.

Jing crouched down beside him. "I know what it's like to miss home," he said, his voice filled with pity. "Why don't you come with me? You can work for me, and I will pay you. I cannot offer you a Kingdom-Under-the-Sea, but I have a fish pond, large enough for you to swim in..."

"Thank you," Jiaoren replied. "For a few hours at a time, my tail will transform to legs, and I can earn my keep. Then I need to return to the water to swim and to sleep."

On those words, Jiaoren rose from the ground.

To Jing's surprise, he saw a pair of legs, as green as the seaweed hair, in place of the fish's tail. And then, together, they headed off to the mountain village that Jing called home.

Jing was delighted to settle back into his little house. His unusual new friend made himself comfortable too. In the evenings, as Jing relaxed beside the fish pond, he watched, fascinated, as Jiaoren slipped into the still waters. As he swam, his long silver tail appeared again, splashing up out of the water.

Jing wondered what his fish made of this strange creature, joining them in their home. And he wondered, too, what Jiaoren made of life on land.

"I miss my home," Jiaoren replied simply. "But I *am* grateful. And one day," he promised, "I will find a way to repay you."

The summer passed and, with the cooling of the air, a change came over Jing. He spent more time away from home, and when he came back, he was distracted, often gazing for hours at a time at the still waters of the fish pond. There was a longing in his expression, and it made Jiaoren think of his own longing for home.

"What is it?" Jiaoren asked Jing at last. "Tell me. I know something has happened and I wish to help you, as you helped me."

In reply, Jing gave a wry smile. "I'm in love," he said, with a sigh.

"But that's wonderful!"

"It's hopeless," said Jing. "I met her at the temple, praying. She goes there with her mother each week. She has the kindest eyes! I knew as soon as I saw her. She looked at me and smiled back. For weeks we looked and smiled, and then, at last, I followed her and her mother home. I wanted to ask her if we could get to know each other better..."

"Go on..." prompted Jiaoren.

"She lives down a narrow alley, in a shabby-looking house, right at the end. I found out that they moved there three years ago, when the girl's father died. They are very poor. They have struggled. I thought my suit would be welcome. I knocked on the door..."

"And?" asked Jiaoren.

"Her mother answered. I said I wanted to talk to her daughter. The daughter smiled. My heart lifted! And then the mother shook her head.

'*My daughter's name is Wanzhu,*' she said. '*Do you know what that means? 10,000 pearls! Bring me 10,000 pearls. Only then will I even consider letting my daughter get to know you.*' And with that, she slammed the door in my face."

"10,000 pearls," repeated Jiaoren.

"I know," said Jing. "Hopeless! How could I ever find that many pearls? Even if I sold my house, all my belongings, my beautiful fish, I couldn't come close to affording them. I must forget Wanzhu, and yet, I can't..."

Over the next few weeks, Jiaoren saw Jing fall deeper and deeper into his sadness. He grew weaker and weaker. The doctor came. He said there was nothing he could do. No medicine could cure a broken heart.

Once the doctor had left, Jiaoren began to cry. "I feel so hopeless," he said. "I'd give anything to be able to help you."

Jing wanted to comfort his friend, but he could only watch as the tears rolled down Jiaoren's cheeks. The tears fell to the floor, glistening, like tiny drops of dew. And then, they began to crystallize, growing rounder, harder – luminescent.

"They're pearls!" whispered Jing. "Your tears are turning to pearls!"

"Of course," said Jiaoren, leaping after them, gathering up the shining jewels in his hands. "I had forgotten. When mermen cry – when they are on land, when they have lost their home – their tears turn to pearls."

Jiaoren had stopped crying now. His mind was racing. "My sorrow can be your joy," he said. "I can give you 10,000 pearls. Take me to the ocean..."

That night, as the moon came up and the stars shone through the darkness, Jiaoren sat on the stony shore where Jing had first found him, and wept 10,000 tears. They flowed freely as he thought of his home, his family, all the merfolk he had loved and lost. And Jing was there beside him, catching the tears in a basket as they turned to pearls under the moonlight.

Jiaoren sat on the stony shore where Jing had first found him, and wept 10,000 tears.

"Stop," said Jing at last. "We have enough. And I cannot bear to see you cry any more."

Jiaoren turned to his friend. "And I cannot stay here any longer. I'll never forget how you took me in, when I had nowhere else to go, but I have repaid my debt to you. Now it is time for me to return to my Kingdom-Under-the-Sea. I have been banished, but I will beg for forgiveness. I will do whatever it takes. My heart yearns for home as yours yearns for love. I want to go back to where I belong."

"I'll never forget you," said Jing.

As the tide rolled in, Jiaoren dived into the water, his seaweed hair trailing behind him. For one last time, Jing watched the silver fish tail rise above the waves, then disappear into the darkness below.

Alone, Jing returned to his mountain village, carrying his basket of shining pearls, each one like a little round moon.

By dawn, Jing reached the shabby house at the end of the narrow alley, and knocked on the door.

Knock, knock, knock. His heart leaped in time, and the door swung open.

"You again!" said Wanzhu's mother, only this time she was smiling.

"At last, I have found a way," said Jing. "I have brought you 10,000 pearls." And he held out his basket, full to the brim. "May I get to know your daughter now?" he asked. "If she would like to know me, of course."

"The pearls are beautiful," said the mother. "But it was only a test, to see how much you truly wished to know my daughter. Now, without doubt, you have earned that right."

The mother stepped aside, and there was Wanzhu, smiling shyly, her eyes as kind as ever.

"Shall we go for a walk?" said Wanzhu.

Days turned to weeks, weeks turned to months, and all that time, Jing and Wanzhu walked together along the lush mountain paths, talking until the sun set low in the sky. Among other things, Jing told Wanzhu of Jiaoren, and the gift of his tears.

Soon, it was clear to everyone that they were deeply in love. The following summer, they were married at the temple where they had first met. And everyone gasped at Wanzhu's wedding dress, which shone with thousands of tiny pearls.

"How many?" whispered the guests.

"10,000," Wanzhu's mother replied.

As for Jioaren... whenever Jing walked along the coast, he looked for him. Sometimes he thought he saw a silver fish's tail, splashing amongst the foam. When he saw the moon, gleaming pearl-like on the dark waters, he remembered him.

"I hope you are forgiven, and as happy as you made me," he whispered across the waves. "I hope you are home again, working your loom, weaving the finest silks under the sea."

Sirena is a sea creature from Philippine mythology. This story has its roots in both Spanish folklore and the Chamorro people of Guam. It is around 200 years old.

Sirena

Many years ago, on the island of Guam, where the mouth of the Hagåtña river meets the ocean, there lived a young girl. Her name was Sirena and she loved the water. Every day, without fail, she would swim in the river, silver-scaled fish darting around her as she dived beneath the surface.

But as she swam, joyful and carefree, Sirena was not where she was *meant* to be, helping her family with the daily chores – cooking, weaving and washing clothes. She did her best to work hard and to help, but whatever task her mother set her, she would quickly abandon to swim in the cool water of the river.

"Sirena, I'm warning you!" her mother, Taitasi, would say. But it made no difference... until the day of the great village feast, in celebration of the harvest.

All morning, Taitasi worked hard. She boiled breadfruit in coconut milk, until it was golden and soft. There was chicken and corn soup, pickled papaya and crab chalakiles. Her children bustled around her, all helping – cooking, stirring, washing, pounding. All that is, except Sirena, who was nowhere to be seen. Only when her youngest sister went down to the river to collect water, did she find Sirena, splashing her feet in the shallows.

"Sirena!" she called. "Come back to the house. Mama is getting angry."

Sirena sighed, reluctant to leave. "I'll come soon," she promised, as her sister began to trudge back towards the house. "I'll be right behind you."

But the sun was so hot, and the water was so refreshing, that Sirena promised herself just one last swim...

When she finally returned home, her mother was furious. "There you are! I've been looking everywhere for you! Where have you—" Her gaze settled on Sirena's long, black hair, dripping with river water. "Swimming. *Again*, Sirena! What am I going to do with you?"

Sirena's face flushed. "I'm very sorry, Mama," she murmured.

"Well, you're here now," said her mother, her tone softening. "Take this basket to your godmother's house and fill it with coal. I still need to cook the fish for the feast tonight and the coal is running low. And remember, come straight back. No swimming, Sirena! Do you hear me?"

Nodding, promising, Sirena took off down the sandy path, feeling determined. "Go to Godmother's," she told herself, "get the coal, come straight back." She chanted the words in her head, over and over, as if that would make them come true.

As Sirena walked, the day became hotter and the air more humid. Ahead, she could see the river winding its way through the undergrowth, its water glinting and sparkling beneath the trees.

All around her birds sang and insects buzzed and churred.

Butterflies flitted in search of flowers and geckos skittered across the jungle floor. It felt as if the jungle were calling to her, as if the river itself were beckoning her. *"Swim, swim,"* it seemed to sing, gurgling by her side.

"Maybe just for a moment," Sirena thought, smiling, unable to resist.

She left the path and made her way to the riverbank, setting down her basket, dipping her feet in the cool water.

Something tickled Sirena's toes and, giggling, she looked down to see a group of shrimp, gathering around her feet. They waved their feather-light tentacles, as if inviting her to join them.

It was all too much... a moment later, Sirena was striding into the river, arms outstretched, submerging herself in the glistening water. The river flowed around her, embracing her, carrying her to its deepest

*She dived down, again and again, delighting in the little fish,
the streaming water weeds, the turtles basking on the rocks.*

part, where her feet barely touched the sandy bottom.

She dived down, again and again, delighting in the little fish, the streaming water weeds, the turtles basking on the rocks.

"Now I will go to Godmother's," Sirena thought, pulling herself from the water one last time. But as she looked around, the jungle was not as she had left it... there was no cacophony of sound. The birds were silent; the chatter of insects had faded to a quiet murmur.

Sirena felt a whoosh of air, and there, rushing past her ear, was a fruit bat, heading for the shadowy trees. Above her, the sky was no longer a bright blue, but had turned a dusky purple, and she saw the sun was dipping fast.

"Oh, no, no, no!" Sirena cried aloud. "I've wasted the whole day!"

She hurried up the riverbank, snatching up the

basket her mother had given her. In the dim light it looked emptier than ever. Sirena began to cry. "There's no time to go to Godmother's now. I can't cross the jungle in the dark. Mama will be so angry with me!"

But there was nothing she could do. Cloaked in darkness, Sirena quietly made her way home. She tiptoed up to the doorway and peeked inside. The house was empty. "Everyone must be at the feast by now," she thought. "Perhaps I can slip in, unnoticed..."

"Sirena!" Her mother's voice cut through the darkness as she emerged from the house, lantern in hand, Sirena's godmother at her side.

"You selfish, idle child!" Anger burned in Taitasi's eyes.

"Your five-year-old sister is more responsible than you. I had to walk over to your godmother's house and collect the coal myself! I don't know *what* to do with you!"

Sirena's gaze fell to the ground, unable to look either her mother or her godmother in the eye. Then her mother's voice dropped dangerously low.

"If you love the water so much," she said slowly, her words hanging thick and heavy in the air, "you're better off living as a fish!"

Sirena began to sob. She knew what would happen now. A mother's words to her daughter carried great power. There was no escape from this.

Through her tears, Sirena saw her mother's face crumple. Her words, no sooner spoken, were deeply regretted.

"Taitasi, no!" her godmother cried. "You've cursed her. And a mother's curse can *never* be undone!"

Taitasi stumbled forwards to hug her daughter, to hold her close, but already Sirena was running down the path, towards the river.

"Wait!" her mother called, racing after her. "Sirena, wait! Don't go! Please, don't go! I didn't mean it! I–"

But the night wind whipped away her words. And Sirena ran on, too fast for her mother as she flitted through the darkness, down the twisting jungle paths.

On her knees, Sirena's godmother implored the spirits of their ancestors for help. "Oh spirits, *Taotao mo'na*, hear my words. Save our sweet Sirena. I beg you, do not let her become a fish. Dim the power of Taitasi's curse!"

By now, Sirena had reached the river. Out of breath, she leaned against a swaying palm tree. Hot tears streamed down her cheeks. The moon was rising above the trees, the water lapped gently at the riverbank. All was silent, but for Sirena's gentle sobbing. Once more, the river called to her, pulling her closer to the water's edge. *"You belong here Sirena. You belong to the river,"* it whispered. *"Just one more step and you will never have to leave the water again."*

Try as she might, Sirena couldn't fight the call of the river, the pull of the water. Its hold on her was stronger than ever. She took a step forward and with one swift, graceful motion, dived into the river.

Her mother arrived just as Sirena disappeared beneath the surface.

This time, the river carried Sirena beyond its quiet, deep pools, all the way in its rushing arms to the ocean. And as the tide came in, as the water turned thick with salt, Sirena began to transform. Scales, shimmering scales, covered her legs, which merged together, bound as one as she spun in the water.

A fin fanned out around her feet, with delicate waving edges.

And now, clearly, looking down, she saw she had a tail – long, pearlescent, shining, sleek as a dolphin's, silver as a fish. It stretched all the way from her waist to where her toes had once been. Tentatively, Sirena reached down to touch it.

"Any moment now," she thought, too amazed to be afraid, "my hands will become fins. Then I will truly be a fish." But the transformation did not come. Sirena touched her face, her arms, ran her fingers through her long hair. Her godmother's plea had been answered. The power of the curse had been dimmed.

Sirena rose above the surface and gazed, once, longingly back at the shore. "Goodbye, Mother. Goodbye, Godmother," she called. Then she slipped beneath the waves. This was her home now...

On the riverbank, Sirena's mother heard her whisper of goodbye, carried all the way from the ocean. She knew she would never see her daughter again.

But every year after that, on the village feast day, a basket of coal would appear on the riverbank, in the exact same spot Sirena had dived for a last time into the water.

The Yara is a river mermaid, originally part of the
ancient mythology of the Tupi and Guaraní tribes in Brazil.

Alonzo and the Yara

*T*he summer Alonzo and Julia first met was the hottest anyone could remember. It's true, summers were always hot in that part of the world – far hotter than where Alonzo had grown up. But this year, for months on end, it was too hot to do anything.

People slept all day, if they could. Sometimes it felt as if the whole world were half asleep. But life still went on, and on the hottest day of all, as it happened, the town came together for a grand celebratory feast.

Alonzo saw Julia before she saw him. She stood out from the crowd, in her white dress, with red flowers in her hair. He thought her the most beautiful girl he had ever seen. And if you asked Julia, she would tell you that Alonzo was the most handsome boy in the world. They talked all evening and into the early hours, and parted with a promise to meet again the very next day.

From then on, Alonzo visited Julia every evening after he'd finished work. They spent hours in Julia's garden, laughing and talking until the stars came out, or sometimes just sitting in silence, holding hands and watching the hummingbirds dart from flower to flower. Before long, they became engaged to be

married, and it seemed that nothing could spoil
their happiness.

But one day, after visiting Julia, Alonzo decided
to walk by the river at the edge of the forest. He
was halfway home when he discovered the pool. Its
waters were crystal clear and, where the water lapped
lazily at its edges, you could see every pebble on the
bottom. Towards the middle, though, the water was
so deep, it was as dark and still as a moonless night.

Alonzo barely hesitated before throwing off his
clothes and wading in. It was just as refreshingly cool

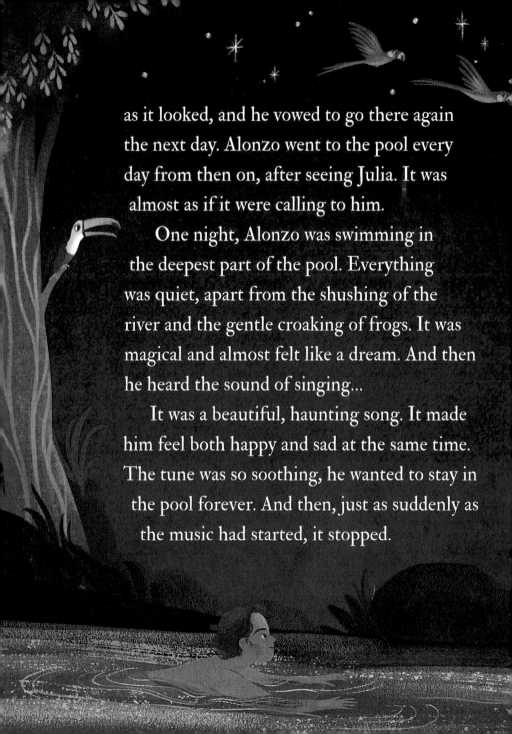

as it looked, and he vowed to go there again
the next day. Alonzo went to the pool every
day from then on, after seeing Julia. It was
almost as if it were calling to him.

One night, Alonzo was swimming in
the deepest part of the pool. Everything
was quiet, apart from the shushing of the
river and the gentle croaking of frogs. It was
magical and almost felt like a dream. And then
he heard the sound of singing...

It was a beautiful, haunting song. It made
him feel both happy and sad at the same time.
The tune was so soothing, he wanted to stay in
the pool forever. And then, just as suddenly as
the music had started, it stopped.

Alonzo thought he saw a flash of something on the bank. He quickly swam over to see who was there, but there was no movement. No sound. Nothing.

The next evening, Alonzo visited Julia as usual. He was just about to leave, when out of the blue, she asked him, "Where did you go after you left me last night, Alonzo?"

Alonzo was surprised, but readily replied, "I went for a swim, as I usually do. There's a beautiful deep pool down by the river. Do you know it?"

Julia shook her head, but her smile had gone now.

"It's so cool and still," Alonzo continued. "I can hardly believe no one else goes there.

Last night, though, the strangest thing happened. I thought I heard singing. It was the sweetest song, although I couldn't make out the words. But there was no one else there! I suppose I must have been dreaming... Whatever's the matter, Julia?"

Julia had gone deathly pale.

"You must promise me," she said, her voice trembling, "never, *ever*, to go to that pool again."

"But... why? I don't understand," Alonzo replied, frowning as he spoke.

"You are not from around here, so you may not have heard the stories about the river."

Alonzo shook his head.

"People say," Julia continued, "that a terrible creature lives in its waters, who preys on young men who are about to be married. She draws them to her with her song, then drags them down under the water to their deaths. She is known as the Yara."

"But surely you don't believe in such things?" protested Alonzo.

Julia shook her head. "I don't know, but just in case... please, don't go there again, Alonzo. If it is her song that you heard, the next time you go there, you will see her, and that can only end in one way – your death."

Alonzo began to laugh.

He knew it was unkind, but he couldn't seem to help it. It was a sharp, harsh laugh that sounded strange even to his own ears and, oddly, he found it hard to stop once he had started.

Julia shuddered.

"You've already seen her, haven't you?" she said dully, drawing away from him.

Alonzo shook his head – he was sure he hadn't, unless that flash on the bank was her – but he was still unable to stop laughing. Julia shrank back further. She had heard that people who'd seen the Yara laughed like this, and, although she tried hard not to, she began to cry. This, at least, finally caused Alonzo to stop.

"I won't go again if it upsets you so," he said. He didn't believe in the Yara, but he loved Julia so much he would do anything for her... Although the thought of never going to the pool again... But, no. He would not go, if that was what she wanted.

"Thank you," Julia replied softly. "But the Yara is very powerful. If she has set her sights on you, she'll call to you, and it will be hard to stop yourself from going. I want you to take something..."

Julia rushed inside the house and returned with a small shell. She then sang softly into it and held it out to him.

"Take this," she said. "If the Yara sings to you
again, hold it to your ear and you will hear my song.
Perhaps my voice will be stronger than hers, and it
will save you."

That night, Alonzo kept his promise and went
straight home. The next night, it was very hot, and
he couldn't help thinking about the pool, how cool
and inviting it was... and for a moment, a wordless
song sang softly in his head. But still he didn't go.
The third night, the song was louder and sweeter, and
he found himself going home by the edge of forest.
But still, he did not venture any closer. But on the
fourth night, the song in his head was so loud and so
heartachingly beautiful – it was almost as if his feet
took him to the pool of their own accord...

Alonzo felt a shiver of fear run through him
when he arrived at the water's edge. He also had an
unshakeable feeling that someone was watching him.

Alonzo was about to wade into the pool when a rustling in the undergrowth made him turn around. And there she was. A beautiful woman with copper skin and dark green hair, half hidden by the ferns.

"The Yara!" thought Alonzo. And Julia's words rang in his head. *She drags men down to their deaths.* Alonzo ran then, as fast as he could, not daring even to look over his shoulder in case it slowed him down.

The next morning, his courage returned and he went to the pool before work to search for any sign of the woman. There was none. "I'm such a fool," he said to himself. "I let fear get the better of me and imagined it all."

He found it hard to concentrate on anything for the rest of the day. He was determined not to go back to the pool, yet at the same time, counted every hour, every minute until he could return. He left Julia early that night, pretending he had a headache.

She watched him go, feeling sick with fear. It was clear to her that something had happened, but when she asked, he had refused to answer her.

As soon as Alonzo had left Julia's sight, he ran all the way to the pool. At first, he was on edge. Every parrot squawk, every lizard scuttling, every whisper of a leaf, had him wheeling around in case it was the green-haired woman. But eventually he began to relax, and even to feel drowsy. He leaned against a tree and must have fallen asleep because he awoke with a start.

"Alonzo. Aloooonzooooo..." a female voice whispered.

He felt his eyes drawn towards the pool. He couldn't tear his eyes away from it. Then a bright spark of light appeared in the deepest, darkest part of the water. The light began to grow

bigger and brighter, and a green mist shimmered
in the night air. Alonzo was terrified, but still, he
couldn't stop looking. Then the waters began to part,
and the same beautiful woman from the night before
rose to the surface. She smiled at Alonzo and, holding
out her arms, she came towards him.

Alonzo tried to run, but his feet were rooted to
the ground. The Yara was coming closer and closer,
her long hair swaying, and her eyes locked on his.

"Stop!" Alonzo cried out. "Don't come any
nearer! *Please!*"

But his voice was weak and feeble.

When the Yara finally reached him, she smiled,
then began to sing – and oh, such a lovely song!
It floated through the trees, it filled the air, it filled
Alonzo's head until he could think of nothing else.
His arms dropped to his sides and he felt all his
strength drain away.

Then the waters began to part, and the same beautiful woman from the night before rose to the surface.

"This is it," he thought, as her song swept over him. "Nothing can save me now." But there was something niggling at the back of his mind... What was he forgetting? Of course! *Julia's shell.* With immense effort, he took it out from his pocket and, unable even to lift it up to his ear, bent his head down to it.

For a moment, the Yara's song grew even louder and sweeter. Alonzo became so weak, he almost fell to his knees, but he held on tightly to the shell. Then, as soft as a whisper, came Julia's voice. At first, he could hardly hear it, but gradually it became stronger and clearer and, as he listened, Alonzo's mind became clearer too. He felt his strength return, and when he lifted his head to look around him, he was alone. The swirling mist had gone and, with it, the Yara. The only song in the air now was the whirring of cicadas and the gurgling of the river.

Alonzo and Julia were married a month later. Julia promised him that now they were married, he was safe from the Yara. But Alonzo was never again tempted to go to the pool, even on the hottest of days – and he always kept Julia's shell in his pocket, just in case...

Stories about Melusine were first told in medieval times in Northern Europe, in countries such as France and Luxembourg.

Melusine

Melusine dipped her feet in the cool, clear water of the fountain, and sighed. In all the wide forest, this fountain – magic, secret, hidden – was the place she loved most. But she still missed her home, the Isle of Avalon, where she'd lived with her family and all the other fairy folk.

But then, one terrible day, her mother had turned against her. She had cursed her and sent her away as punishment, and now here she was, treated like a queen by the fairies of the forest, but so very far from the land she loved.

A loud noise dragged Melusine from her thoughts. Something, or someone, was crashing through the forest. The next moment, a young man staggered into the clearing. When he saw the fountain, he rushed over and drank thirstily. He didn't even notice Melusine at first. But when, at last, he did look up and see her, his expression changed to surprise, then wonder...

He had heard there were magical creatures in the forest, although he'd never believed it. If it *were* true, he thought, she must be one of them. Her long red hair shone like fire and her dark eyes made him think of forest pools, green and glittering. He could swear, too, that when he looked away for a moment, out of the corner of his eye she almost seemed to glow, with a faint watery light of her own.

Melusine broke the silence first. "Are you hurt?" she asked, looking at a cut on his forehead.

"It's nothing," the man replied, wiping some blood away. "My horse threw me off and galloped away. I'm fine, but... *who are you?*"

"I think perhaps you should introduce yourself, first," Melusine replied, smiling.

"Please forgive my rudeness. I am Raymond, Duke of Lusignan. I live in the castle on the other side of the forest." He bowed low. "At your service."

Melusine curtseyed in return. "I am Melusine,"

she said. Then, looking with concern at his cut, she pointed at the fountain. "This water has magical powers. If you wash your forehead with it, your cut will be healed."

"Thank you," Raymond replied, looking doubtful. But he did as she suggested and the cut disappeared.

"Is it true then?" he gasped. "Is there magic in this forest?"

"Why yes," laughed Melusine. "Didn't you know? It's full of fairy folk."

Raymond couldn't tell if she were teasing him, but it didn't matter... Nothing mattered... He was entranced by her, as surely as if he'd been enchanted by a spell. They talked, and time passed strangely quickly. Before Raymond knew it, the sun was setting, and it was time to go.

"May I come back tomorrow?" he asked. "Will you be here?"

"I will," Melusine replied, smiling.

Raymond came back not just the next day, but the one after that, and every single day for the next few months. And before long, they were both very much in love. When Raymond proposed, Melusine's heart leaped... But then she remembered her mother's curse and her happiness was swiftly replaced by worry.

"I would love to marry you," she told Raymond, "but before I can say yes, you must make me a promise."

"*Anything*," Raymond replied.

Melusine took a deep breath. "Can you swear to me that, once we are married, you will let me spend each Saturday evening alone?"

"Is that all?" Raymond laughed. "Of course!"

"You must not even *try* to see me," Melusine continued earnestly.

"I promise! I shall spend my evening in an entirely different part of the castle, if you so wish it."

"Raymond," said Melusine, "I want you to understand – this is very important. If you break this promise, I must leave you, and we will both be miserable for the rest of our lives."

"I will never betray your trust," said Raymond, serious now, "any more than I will ever stop loving you, whatever happens."

"Then, yes! I will marry you!" Melusine declared, her face lit up with joy.

That evening, after Raymond had gone, Melusine waited until she was sure she was alone, then slipped into the waters of the fountain.

First came the familiar tingling sensation in her legs. And then, her skin began to shimmer, turning a luminous, glimmering green, that reflected the light like the wings of a dragonfly. Next, her toes fanned out, and her legs became longer, rippling, scaling... until they had transformed into two fish-like tails.

*Next, her toes fanned out, and her legs became longer, rippling, scaling...
until they had transformed into two fish-like tails.*

For this was Melusine's curse – or at least a part of it. Once a week, for a few hours, she became a mermaid. And she must, at all costs, keep it a secret from her beloved. What would he think of her if he knew? And the rest of the curse? She could only pray it would never come to pass.

Raymond and Melusine were married in spring by the fountain where they had first met. The fairies of the forest watched from behind the trees, silently wishing the couple luck. The fairies knew all too well that marriages between fairies and humans rarely ended happily...

But for many years, the marriage *was* a joyful one. Raymond and Melusine had many children, and their love for each other never waned. Together, they ruled their people wisely and well. Their kingdom prospered and their people were contented.

Raymond faithfully kept the promise he'd made to Melusine. Once a week, she withdrew to their rooms, and he spent the evening elsewhere in the castle. He never questioned her, or asked her to release him from his promise. He loved and respected her far too much to do so. And if, from time to time, he couldn't help wondering about his mysterious wife, he quickly put those thoughts to one side.

Time passed. Their children grew up and left home. And then, one day, Raymond's cousin came to stay. He saw Raymond and Melusine's love for each other and how it seemed to grow stronger each day, and he was filled with jealousy. He longed to drive a wedge between them.

"Why is it, Raymond," he asked, in a wheedling tone, "that you're not allowed in your own rooms tonight? Is it *just* because your wife says so?"

"It's no sacrifice," Raymond replied.

"But don't you wonder what she's doing in there? Don't you ever feel a little jealous?"

"Why on earth should I feel jealous?" Raymond asked, laughing.

His cousin just shrugged, and Raymond decided to pay him no more attention. But a seed of doubt had been sown, and it quickly took root. As the days passed, he found himself longing for an answer.

The next Saturday evening, Raymond left dinner early, saying that he was going for a walk. But he didn't leave the castle. Instead, he went up to the rooms he shared with his wife, hid behind a screen, and waited.

Before long, Melusine arrived, along with an army of servants carrying a large bathtub and buckets of water. As soon as the servants had filled the tub, they left, and Melusine climbed into the bath and sank down into the water with a long sigh.

"I'm such a fool," thought Raymond, ashamed of himself. "Of course! She's just bathing and having time alone. What else would she be doing?"

But then came a loud SPLASH, and two large scaly tails flopped over the edge of the bathtub. Raymond stood on tiptoes, peering closer... and gasped. His wife had become a mermaid!

Raymond crept from the room, as quietly as he could, desperately hoping Melusine had not heard him. He felt sad that she'd kept this secret from him. Nothing could make him love her less. But he felt sorrier still that he'd broken his promise. He decided she need never know. But the secret turned out to be too big for him to keep...

One hot summer's day, two of their sons came home to visit, and had a terrible argument.

Raymond was so angry with them that he lost his

temper. Melusine tried to calm him down, but this only made things worse.

"This is all your fault," he shouted at her. "Get away from me, you, you... *foul fish*!"

The moment he said it, Melusine knew that he had spied on her. She ran from the room in tears.

Raymond ran after her, but Melusine turned on him.

"You have broken your promise," she said, "but I must keep mine. As you have seen, I am cursed. But my curse is not just to become a mermaid. It is also that if I marry and discover that my husband has betrayed me, I shall become a shadow, a ghost – a wraith-like being, more spirit than flesh..."

"I... I'm so sorry..." Raymond began. "Surely we can find a way to break this curse?"

Melusine shook her head sadly. "It has already begun," she replied. "And when it is complete, I must leave you."

"Will I ever see you again?" Raymond asked.

"A week before your death," Melusine replied. "I will appear to you again for a brief time. There is nothing else I can do. I must say farewell, my love."

"Please, don't go," said Raymond, reaching out for her. But already, she had begun to fade, her body shimmering at the edges with a faint green light, her eyes brimming with tears.

"I'm sorry. It's too late," Melusine whispered.

By now, her body was made more of air than substance. She was disappearing from the room like shadows under the midday sun.

Once more, Raymond tried to reach for her, but his arms swept through her and he fell to the floor. When he looked up again, she had gone.

Raymond buried his face in his hands. "No..." he whimpered.

He stayed on the cold floor all night, too full of grief to move or even to notice the passing of time. When he finally lifted his head again, another day was dawning, the first light slanting in through the castle windows.

Raymond got to his feet unsteadily and called his sons to him. He told them what had happened. "You have only me to blame," he said.

After that, Raymond closed up his castle and refused to see anyone but the servants. All he could long for now was the day he would see his beloved Melusine again.

The years passed and, at the end, Melusine kept

her promise. The week before Raymond died, she came to him. His face lit with joy at the sight of her.

"I have come to say one last goodbye, my love," she said, shimmering at his side. "I forgive you. What you did cannot be undone, but we had many happy years."

"Now I will die in peace," said Raymond, "for I have seen you one last time."

The story does not end there. Ever since that day, it is said Melusine has appeared near the castle whenever a duke is close to death. And so the legend of Melusine and Raymond lives on...

This fairy tale, about seal folk or selkies, comes from the north of Scotland, near John O' Groats.

The Seal Catcher

*O*nce there was a seal catcher who lived right at the very top of Scotland, in a cottage by the sea. Not far from her house, the seals would pull themselves up on the rocks of the Pentland Firth, and bathe in the sun. The seal catcher would go down to the beach each day, and lie in wait for the big, sleek seals to come.

If she was lucky, she would catch one and skin it, then sell the skin to feed herself and her children. Her husband had died the year before and she had no one else to help her. But nor did she need any help. She had become so skilled at catching seals that she was known as *The Greatest Seal Catcher in the North.*

Sometimes, people would say to her, "Beware the biggest seals, for they are selkie folk. They come from a kingdom of their own, deep down under the waves, and can take on human form. Once a month, when the moon is full, they cast off their skin and dance in the moonlight."

The seal catcher scoffed at them. "I don't believe in your moonshine talk," she said. And she went on with her trade, catching the seals as they lay basking on the rocks.

But then one day... perhaps the seal catcher was too slow... or perhaps she slipped on the rocks... but as she struck a seal it dived away before she could catch it, back into the stormy sea, carrying her knife along with it.

The seal catcher lunged after it, but the seal was too fast for her, and the sea too wild to think of diving into the water. So the seal catcher turned to go home, fretting over the loss of her knife. She climbed the rocky cliff path, and began the journey back.

It had been a clear day when she set out, but now a thick mist billowed in from the sea. It clung to her hair in salty drops and snaked, ghost-like, around her legs. Then, in the distance, she heard the sound of galloping hooves, so heavy the ground began to tremble. The seal catcher stopped and stood to one side, her heart beating fast, though she couldn't say why.

A moment later, a great black horse
appeared out of the mist, with a
stranger riding on it. The horse
was bigger than any horse
she had seen before, and the
stranger was bigger than any
man she had seen before, with
huge dark eyes, as black as the
ocean on a starless night.

"Good day," said the stranger. "What
are you doing out in this mist, so close to the rocks
and the raging sea?"

"I'm a seal catcher," she replied. "And I'm on my
way home."

"Ah!" said the stranger, smiling in delight. "Then
I am lucky to have found you. I would like to order
a hundred seal skins and I can pay you in gold. But
I will need them by tonight."

"I cannot help you," said the seal catcher, her voice full of disappointment. "The seals have gone now, and won't return to the rocks until the morning."

"But I can help *you*," replied the stranger. "I know a place thick with seals, more than you will have ever seen before. Climb up onto my horse and I'll take you there."

The seal catcher hesitated. There was something about the stranger that held her back. Perhaps it was the look in his eyes, or the lilt of his voice, that seemed to wash over her in waves... but the thought of all that gold, and how it could feed and clothe her children, was too tempting to refuse. So she climbed up behind the rider, and off galloped the great horse.

They sped like the wind down the narrow cliff path. On and on they went. The sea mist swirled around them, closer and closer, until the seal catcher lost track of where they were and where they were going.

At last, the rider pulled on the reins, and the mist

cleared enough for her to see they had stopped, right at the edge of a precipice, with dark rocks that fell away to the sea far below.

"Get down now," said the stranger, abruptly, and the seal catcher did as she was asked.

She gazed down at the cliff, but saw no rocks below her, only the churning sea. "Where are the seals?" she asked, nervously, wishing she had never set out with the stranger.

"You'll soon see," said the stranger. The next moment, he placed his hands on the seal catcher's shoulders and then she was falling, falling, so fast the wind whipped her voice away, even as she called for help.

She fell far and fast, down to the sea below, hitting the water with a great SPLASH! She felt the dark waters close over her head. "This is it," she thought to herself. "This is it..."

But then, to her amazement, she found she could breathe easily, and the water felt warm and silky soft against her skin. She could feel the weight of the stranger in the water above her, and they plummeted down together, deeper and deeper, just as quickly as they had flown through the air.

At last, they came to a great arched doorway, and a door, studded with coral and cockleshells, which swung open to reveal a huge, domed hall. The walls were lined with mirrors and studded with mother of pearl. On the floor lay golden sand. And everywhere the seal catcher looked she saw neither fish nor people, but selkies. When she turned to look at the stranger, she saw that he, too, was a selkie, with a seal's face and a seal's body, and a delicate golden crown.

"So all the stories were true," thought the seal catcher. "And all this time, I've been catching selkie folk, and now they'll have their revenge... and this must be it!" she realized, catching sight of her reflection in a mirror. For she was no longer human, but a selkie herself.

She was seal all over – from her soft fur to her flippers to her large dark eyes, staring unblinkingly back at her.

When she turned, she saw the other selkies in the hall, talking between themselves in whispers. Their voices sounded hushed and sad. They moved gently, mournfully. Some lay on the sandy floor, wiping large tears from their eyes with their soft, furry fins.

Then the selkie who had come to her as a stranger on a horse, swam out of the hall and returned, with a knife tucked under his flipper. "Have you seen this before?" he asked.

To her horror, the seal catcher knew it for her own. It was the knife that she had used that morning, that had been carried away by the wounded seal.

When she turned, she saw the other selkies in the hall, talking between themselves in whispers. Their voices sounded hushed and sad.

In reply, the seal catcher could only nod.

"Follow me," said the selkie, and he led the way out of the great hall and into a smaller room. There lay a selkie on a bed of pale green sea lettuce, with a great wound in his side. On his head, he too wore a golden crown.

"That is my father, our king," said the selkie, "the one you wounded this morning. I know you thought he was just another seal of the sea, but he is our ruler. He can speak and understand just as you can. I brought you here to bind his wounds. Only the one who struck him can heal him."

"So you are a prince?" asked the seal catcher. The selkie nodded.

"I have no skills in the art of healing," said the seal catcher. "But I will try my best." And she swam over to the wounded king.

She washed the wound, using a little bowl

beside him, and dressed it with seaweed. To her amazement, her touch was like magic. No sooner had she cleaned the wound, than the old seal seemed to recover.

First the light returned to his eyes, his fur turned from dull and lank to golden brown and then he swam, up from his bed, out of his room and into the great hall. There he twisted and turned, slipping through the water, sleek and fast.

The other seals laughed and clapped and swam after him, rubbing their noses against his with joy.

And all the time, the seal catcher stayed in the corner, fear in her heart. *What would happen now?* Would they punish her by keeping her down here forever as a selkie? She thought of her children, waiting for her at home. Would she only be allowed to come to them once in a full moon, when she could shed her skin and dance on the stony shore?

As she waited, wondering, the selkie prince came to her, and she saw there was no anger in his gaze. "You are free to return to land," he said. "We will not keep you here. I will take you back – but only on one condition."

"And what is that?" asked the seal catcher.

"You must promise never to wound a seal again."

The seal catcher paused only for a moment. She had no idea how she would feed her children, what trade she would take up, but she would do anything to be back with them again. Nor did she think she could ever harm another seal.

"I promise," she said, aloud.

The selkie prince held up his flipper, the seal catcher did the same, and they touched the tips of their flippers together. The other selkies crowded around to witness it.

"Now follow me," said the selkie prince, and he led the seal catcher out of the great hall, through the archway of coral, up and up, rising through the green shadows of the deep.

The water grew lighter as they neared the surface, until, at last, they broke through into the cold, fresh air, back by the shores of the Pentland Firth.

"Go well," said the selkie prince, when the seal catcher had safely reached the rocks. Then he disappeared beneath the waves. The last the seal catcher saw of him were his large, dark eyes, like pools of night, slipping beneath the surface.

When the seal catcher looked down, she saw she was a selkie no more. Instead of her seal fur, she had her own skin. Instead of a tail, there were her legs. And beside her was a brown bag she hadn't noticed before. She picked it up and it felt heavy in her hands – so heavy she could barely lift it. But she dragged it home with her, along the cliff path, all the way back to her cottage.

When she came through the door, her children gathered around her, asking what she had caught that day.

"Nothing," replied the seal catcher, "and I'll never be catching seals again." And she told the children her story.

"But how will we live, Mother?" asked her eldest, when the tale was done, her eyes round with worry.

"I'll find a way," sighed the seal catcher. "Now, let's see what the selkies have given us."

She opened the bag, peered inside, and gasped... for the bag gleamed with gold – enough for the seal catcher and her family to live on for the rest of their lives. And she was true to her word. She never caught a seal again for the remainder of her days.

This story is based on a fairy tale by
Danish author Hans Christian Andersen.
It was first published in 1837.

The Little Mermaid

*L*ong ago, far beneath the surface of the
ocean, lived the merfolk, in a secret world
of their own. They had seashell homes encrusted
with pearls, and gardens of shining sea flowers.
But grandest and most beautiful of all was the
Sea King's palace, which stood among towering
mountains of coral, flanked by seaweed forests.

Here the Sea King lived with his six daughters, who loved nothing more than to tend to the palace gardens. Day by day, they decorated the gardens with hundreds of treasures and trinkets, discovered in the hulls of sunken ships. And at the very heart of the garden stood their most beloved treasure – a marble statue of a human.

Vella, the littlest mermaid, loved this statue most of all. She would spend hours sitting beside it, gazing up at its carved face, wishing and wondering.

Every evening, before bed, the princesses would gather around, combing each other's hair, listening to their grandmother's stories, as she told them of the world above the waves.

"On your 21st birthday, you may go to the surface," she told the princesses. "You will see such incredible things! Ships that glide on the water, human towns, and forests that stretch as far as the eye can see... Just remember, *you* must never be seen!"

The sisters would drink in these stories, eyes round and dreamy, and ask their grandmother question after question. But it was always the littlest mermaid who was the most inquisitive. Even as she was drifting to sleep, she would ask her grandmother to tell her about the human world, only to return to it in her dreams.

Then, at last, Helia, the eldest sister, reached her 21st birthday. She swam to the surface while her sisters waited far below, barely able to contain their excitement.

"What was it like?" they cried out at her return.

"What did you see?"

"Tell us everything!"

"It was beautiful," Helia said. "I lay on a sandbank and bathed in the moonlight! In the distance, the lights from a human town shone like stars."

When Kaia, the next sister, reached her 21st birthday, she, too, swam to the surface, and returned to tell her sisters about the golden sun, burning brightly in the wide arc of the sky.

The following year, Naia, the third sister, returned wreathed in smiles. "I swam up a river! I saw a castle and there were human children playing all around!"

Mira, the fourth sister, spoke of how the water rolled on the surface of the ocean, rising and falling like a giant creature with a life of its own.

And with each passing year, Vella became more and more desperate to see it all for herself.

The fifth sister, Ona, rose to the surface in winter, and came back with tales of a very different world. "Huge chunks of ice floated past me," she said. "White as the northern whales, and sparkling bright like diamonds!"

"I can't wait for *my* birthday!" Vella whispered.

When the day finally came, Vella hugged her sisters and raced to the surface, her tail pounding, her heart thrumming.

"What will it be like?" she wondered.

The sun had almost dipped below the horizon when the Little Mermaid broke the surface. Clouds glowed red and orange. The sky was streaked with gold.

A large ship lay anchored not far from where she had surfaced. The sound of music and singing floated across the water and as the sun disappeared, hundreds of lanterns lit the night.

Unable to contain her curiosity, Vella swam closer. Sailors danced and shouted on the deck above. All of a sudden, a huge cheer went up:

"Happy Birthday, Prince Ari!"

Vella pulled herself onto a rock to see the prince, dressed in white, laughing and hugging his party guests. Enchanted, the Little Mermaid watched the ship all night.

At last, the party came to an end. The chatter sank to a murmur, the guests went to their beds, the lanterns were extinguished. But the sailors were still hard at work. One by one, they unfurled the sails and the ship creaked to life. By now, huge clouds had gathered on the horizon and a strong wind blew over

the ocean's surface, whipping up waves and sending
them surging against the ship's hull. The sailors cried
out as zigzags of lightning ripped across the sky,
turning night to day, great claps of thunder ringing in
their wake.

The sea grew rougher still, inky black waves
surging up like mountains, towering over the ship as
it struggled through the water. Vella gasped as a wave
crashed onto the deck and, with a dreadful groan, the
ship rolled onto its side. Another wave came, and then
another, and the Little Mermaid could only watch
as the ship began to sink, down, down, down into the
water. She caught sight of the prince, thrown free
of the ship, his white shirt shining in the moonlight,
before he too was pulled beneath the waves.

"I must save him," she thought.

Diving under the water, she swam hard and fast
towards Prince Ari. His eyes fluttered shut as Vella

The Little Mermaid

*...Vella grabbed him and pulled him to the surface, allowing
the waves to carry them wherever they chose...*

grabbed him and pulled him to the surface, allowing the waves to carry them wherever they chose...

The next morning, the sun rose bright above a calm, quiet sea. Vella saw land in the distance, nestled in a small bay.

She lay Prince Ari on the soft sand, watching as the sun's rays kissed his pallid cheeks to life. Vella brushed the wet hair from his face. "Please, wake up!" she begged, gently shaking him.

But then she heard voices nearby. Vella slipped back into the shallows and hid behind the rocks. A man and his young daughter came into view. As soon as they saw the prince, they rushed over to him. It wasn't long before Prince Ari woke, and the last Vella saw was the man and his daughter leading Ari up the beach, and out of sight.

The Little Mermaid had no choice but to return home. Her sisters had thought her visit to the surface would finally satisfy her curiosity, but it had only made it stronger.

"There's so much more I have to know about the land above," she told them. "More than I'd ever imagined." And every day, she would ask her grandmother even more questions than before.

"How long do humans live, Grandmother?"

"Their life is short," her grandmother replied. "Usually less than a hundred years. Nothing compared to the three hundred we merfolk live."

"I would gladly live a human lifespan, if it meant I could spend it exploring their world," said the Little Mermaid, looking wistfully at her tail.

"Everything comes with a price, my dear," her grandmother replied. "And you must always ask yourself... is it a price worth paying?" Then she shook her head, and smiled. "No matter though, my love – I doubt even the mighty Sea Witch herself could conjure a spell to give you what you want."

"The Sea Witch?" Vella thought. "Of course! Why didn't I think of that before?" She flung her arms around her grandmother, hugging her tightly. "You're right, Grandmother. Thank you."

That night, while her family slept, Vella set off to visit the Sea Witch's cave, in the darkest part of the ocean. No flowers blossomed here, no sea grass grew. A voice, smooth as silk, whispered in the Little Mermaid's ear. "I know what you want; I know why you're here..." Vella spun around, eyes wide with shock. The Sea Witch stood before her.

"Such a silly wish," the Sea Witch continued,

"but still, I can help you turn that fish's tail into the legs you so desperately desire. Do you want my help?"

"I do," Vella answered.

"Do you realize," asked the Sea Witch, "that once you have human form, you will never be a mermaid again? If you try to return home, you will become no more than foam on the waves."

But still Vella insisted, "I am sure."

"Such certainty!" cackled the Sea Witch. "I will make you a potion, but you must give something of yourself in return. Your voice!"

"No! Not my voice!" Vella gasped.

"Very well then, your hair!" smiled the Sea Witch, coming closer.

Vella looked down at her long, flowing hair, trailing in the water, combed so many times by her sisters. A mermaid's hair meant everything. It was her tie to the ocean itself. Vella gulped... and nodded.

"You may take my hair!" she said.

The sun had not yet risen when the Little Mermaid reached the same small bay where she had left Prince Ari. The moon shone bright in the sky, its light scattering across the water. Vella pulled herself onto shore and shook her cropped hair free of water.

Feeling curiously light-headed, she held up the bubbling potion the Sea Witch had given her, and swallowed it down. No sooner had it touched her lips, than her eyes began to close. The last thing she heard was the gentle suck and tug of the ocean, brushing over the sand...

When Vella opened her eyes again, Prince Ari was standing over her.

"Can I help you?" he asked. "Are you hurt?"

In a rush, it came back to her. Vella looked down. "My tail!" she thought. She gasped. It had gone. In its place, a pair of human legs... just as the Sea Witch had promised.

"Were you shipwrecked?" Ari asked.

Not knowing what else to say, Vella nodded in reply, her eyes round with wonder.

"Please let me help you," said Ari, offering her his hand. "Lean on me," he added, as Vella's new legs wobbled beneath her. Then together, they walked slowly up the beach.

From that day on, Vella and Ari were inseparable.

He brought her to his palace and lent her his clothes.
They ate their meals together, danced together, and
explored the forest paths outside the palace gardens.
And each day, Vella discovered something new about
the human world – a bushy-tailed squirrel bounding
up a tree, the beauty of a butterfly's wings, flowers
with scents she had never imagined. Ari taught her
to ride a horse and soon, it felt as natural to her as
swimming. "I've never felt so free!" she thought,
as they went riding together across vast fields.

One evening, as they sat watching the
sunset in the palace garden, listening
to the last of the day's birdsong,
Ari turned to her. "Vella,"
he said, his voice
shaking a little,
"I am so lucky
to have met you.

These past weeks have been the happiest of my life." Vella's heart fluttered in her chest; she took Ari's hand in her own. "I've fallen in love with you," Ari confessed. "I want to travel the world with you. Promise me we can go exploring together?"

Vella smiled. She clutched his hand... She knew she loved him too, but in that moment, it came to her – all that she had left behind.

"I... I need to think a while," Vella replied. And on those words, she left the prince and ran down to the little bay, and looked out across the rolling waves.

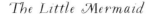

"I will never be with my family again," she realized. Tears rolled down her cheeks and into the ocean.

"Vella! Little sister!" a familiar voice drifted across the water.

"Helia?" Vella saw her oldest sister rise up out of the water, her face full of concern.

"Your tears called me to you," said Helia. "We guessed what you had done. I went to the Sea Witch. She told me everything. Don't worry, little sister. I've persuaded her to help.

In return for my voice, she will make another potion, so that you can regain your tail and return to us."

"Oh, Helia," said Vella, smiling through her tears. "I love you all so much, but do not make such a sacrifice for me. You must never give up your voice. And I *want* to stay here," she went on. "The human world is everything I have dreamed of and more. I've met a man I love. And there is still so much to explore."

"I understand," said Helia, trying to smile. "We want nothing more than for you to be happy. Are you really sure?"

With tears in her eyes, Vella nodded. "Even if it means giving up my life as a mermaid... still, I really am sure."

"We'll miss you," said Helia. "And remember, when you wish to see us, drop a tear into the ocean and we will always come to you."

Then she disappeared beneath the waves once more. Vella stood there for a while, remembering her grandmother's words. *Everything comes with a price, my dear.* The price for her human life was great. She was leaving so much behind, but she was excited, too.

Just then, she heard Prince Ari, calling to her. With one last glance at the ocean, Vella ran to meet him. "Goodbye," she called to the ocean. "And here's to my new life, just beginning..."

Edited by Susanna Davidson
Designed by Tabitha Blore
Series editor: Lesley Sims
Series designer: Russell Punter

Grateful acknowledgements are due to Paria Publishing Co. Ltd., which owns the
copyright of *Ti Jeanne's Last Laundry*, on which our retelling of *Mama Dlo* was based.

First published in 2021 by Usborne Publishing Ltd., Usborne House,
83-85 Saffron Hill, London, EC1N 8RT, England. usborne.com